LAB OF FEAR

WEREWOLF SKIN

by Michael Dahl   illustrated by Igor Šinkovec

raintree

a Capstone company — publishers for children

Raintree is an imprint of Capstone Global Library Limited, a
company incorporated in England and Wales having its registered
office at 7 Pilgrim Street, London, EC4V 6LB – Registered
company number: 6695582

WWW.RAINTREE.CO.UK
myorders@raintree.co.uk

BRITISH LIBRARY CATALOGUING IN PUBLICATION DATA
A full catalogue record for this book is available from the British
Library.

Paperback ISBN: 978-1-4747-0516-5
Ebook ISBN: 978-1-4747-0521-9

19 18 17 16 15
10 9 8 7 6 5 4 3 2 1

DESIGNER: Kristi Carlso

Printed in China

CONTENTS

Grrrrrr!

Lobo! What's wrong?

Is there someone out there in the dark?

Ah, it's only you.

Please, come inside.

Down, Lobo, down!

Poor thing gets excited now and then.

I see you've noticed the animal hide on my wall.

I call it my "Werewolf Skin." Hehe.

There are quite a number of them
in the world...

But mine is special.

Do you want to know *why*?

CHAPTER ONE
IT CAME WITH THE CABIN

Three shadowy figures entered the unlit cabin.

It was a father and his two sons. They had gone to hunt for the weekend.

The boys emptied their rucksacks and
rolled out their sleeping bags. Their father
built a fire in the old stone fireplace.

Soon, the orange flames were crackling.

The younger boy, Lucas, noticed something strange on the floor.

"Is that a bear skin rug?" he asked. "It looks strange."

Their father chuckled.

"That's because it isn't a bear skin," he said.

"It's a <u>wolf</u> skin."

The rug had a wolf's head.

The man held the head closer to the fire.

Orange lights glowed in the wolf's glassy eyes.

The older boy, Travis, asked, "Did your friend kill it?"

Their father shook his head. "No," he said.

He put the wolf skin back on the floor.

"When my friend bought this cabin, the rug was already here," he said.

"In fact," said the father, "he told me this wasn't a wolf skin at all."

Lucas stared at the wolf head's gleaming fangs.

"Then what is it?" he asked.

"A _werewolf_ skin," said his father.

CHAPTER TWO
WEREWOLF TALE

"There's no such thing as werewolves," Travis said.

"That's what my friend thought, too," said their father. "That is, until he shot one in the woods."

Their father's shadow seemed to **grow**. "He had the giant wolf skinned," he said. "He made it into a rug. This rug."

The man leaned back and smiled. "He told me that, sometimes, he could still hear it growling." Grrrrrr Grrrr Grrr

Travis snorted with laughter.

"Nice try, Dad," he said. "That silly story isn't going to scare us."

Lucas's eyes were wide. They reflected the flames of the fire.

"I thought werewolves were people who *turned* into wolves," he said.

"That's right," said his father.

"Then *what* happened to the person who this werewolf used to be?" Lucas asked.

"Maybe he's still here," said his father. He looked down at the rug. "Waiting to come back."

"Don't believe him, Luke," said Travis.

Their father winked. Then he stood up and stretched.

"Time for bed," he announced.

CHAPTER THREE
COVERING UP

Their father went to sleep in the cabin's only bedroom.

The brothers slept in their sleeping bags on sofas in the living area.

The wolf skin lay between them.

In the middle of the night, Lucas woke up shivering.

The fire had gone out.

Travis was still asleep.

He didn't seem bothered by the bitter coldness.

But Lucas could see his own breath in the moonlight.

Lucas looked down at the wolf skin rug.

He reached down and felt it.

He was surprised by how heavy it was.

He covered his sleeping bag with
the wolf's black pelt.

Nice and warm, he thought.

Then he lay back down and closed his eyes.

He dreamt of something **DARK** and **HEAVY** running through the woods.

AawoOooooooOoo

It **HOWLED** at the moon.

The moon was as yellow as a wolf's eye.

CHAPTER FOUR
THE HUNT

At midnight, a fearful howling filled the woods.

Travis woke up with a start.

He saw that the fire had gone out.

The door to the cabin was wide open.

And Lucas was gone.

The **HOWLING** got louder.

Travis ran to the door.

"Lucas!" he cried out.

There was no answer.

He grabbed his rifle and ran into the woods.

The ancient trees echoed with the HOWLING.

Travis couldn't tell where the sounds were coming from.

"*Lucas!*" he shouted again.

I should have told Dad, thought Travis.

But he couldn't go back to the cabin.

His brother was out there in the forest somewhere. All alone.

Travis trudged on. His eyes darted backwards and forwards in the DARK.

Why did Lucas go out in the middle of the night? he wondered.

Did he go outside to see what the howling was about?

Travis saw something crouching next to a tree.

It had yellow eyes.

CHAPTER FIVE
THE RIFLE

The shadow stepped into the moonlight.

Travis was shocked. He almost dropped his rifle.

A beast rose up in front of him.

The beast looked like a **WOLF**.

But it stood on two legs like a human.

It opened its powerful jaws and HOWLED.

Then the wolfish beast crouched,
ready to pounce.

Travis steadied his rifle.

He aimed at the horrible creature.

He pointed his gun at its gleaming
yellow eyes.

A shot rang out.

The **BEAST** screamed and scurried back into the forest.

But Travis hadn't pulled the trigger.

He turned around to see his father standing behind him. Smoke trailed from his father's rifle.

"*Dad!*" Travis shouted. His heart was racing.

"Lucas is missing," he said.

Travis's father nodded. "I know," he said. His eyes were wide with horror. "So is the <u>wolf skin rug</u>."

Poor Lucas was never found.

The werewolf that had been shot
was never found either. Strange, eh?

It probably ran off to die somewhere
in the woods.

All alone.

Maybe.

Down, Lobo, down.

Ah, yes, did you notice the poor creature's limp?

Just don't make any loud noises around him.

He's still a little … <u>gun-shy</u>. Hehe.

PROFESSOR IGOR'S LAB NOTES

People have been telling stories about werewolves since the times of Ancient Greece. Back then, werewolves were called lycanthropes, which means "wolf men" in the Ancient Greek language.

In that story, a king called Lycaon served the god Zeus a dish. But it was no ordinary dish – the evil Lycaon had cooked one of his sons, Nyctimus, into it! Lycaon wanted to see if Zeus really did see and know everything, or if he was lying.

However, Zeus saw right through Lyacoan's plot. As punishment, Zeus revived Nyctimus – and transformed Lycaeon into a wolf! It's thought that this is where the werewolf myth comes from.

Some people believe in werewolves and werewolf-like creatures. Many have claimed to have seen a human-ape beast called Bigfoot. Others have claimed to see Bigfoot's colder cousin, the Yeti (also known as the abominable snowman). In Mexico, the myth of the chupacabra (or "goat sucker" in Spanish) is taken seriously by some. The beast supposedly drinks the blood of goats at night. Yum!

What do you think goes bump in the night?

GLOSSARY

BEAST wild animal that is large, dangerous or unusual

BITTER extreme (as in extremely cold)

BOTHERED caused someone to feel troubled, concerned or annoyed

CRACKLING short, sharp noises

GLEAMING bright or shining

PELT skin or fur of a dead animal

POUNCE suddenly jump towards and take hold of something

RIFLE gun with a long barrel. It is held against the shoulder when fired.

SCURRIED moved quickly (often in fear) with short steps

SHINING producing or reflecting a bright light

STEADIED held firmly in position

DISCUSSION QUESTIONS

1. Was the boys' father telling the truth about the rug? Why or why not?

2. What do you think happened to Lucas? Where is he now?

3. Why do you think the father's eyes went wide at the end of the book? What did he realize? How do you know?

WRITING PROMPTS

1. Write your own short story about a scary werewolf. Make sure you add a spooky twist or surprise to the ending.

2. Werewolves are popular mythical creatures. Create your own scary beast. What kind of monster is it? What does it look like? Why is it dangerous?

3. Have you ever stayed in a cabin? If so, write about your experience. If not, write about the kind of cabin you'd like to stay in.

AUTHOR BIOGRAPHY

Michael Dahl, the author of the Library of Doom, Dragonblood and Troll Hunters series, has a long list of things he's afraid of: dark rooms, small rooms, damp rooms (all of which describe his writing area), storms, rabid squirrels, wet paper, raisins, flying in planes (especially taking off, cruising and landing) and creepy dolls. He hopes that by writing about fear he will eventually be able to overcome his own. So far it isn't working. But he is afraid to stop, so he continues to write. He lives in a haunted house in Minnesota, USA.

ILLUSTRATOR BIOGRAPHY

Igor Sinkovec was born in Slovenia in 1978. As a child he dreamt of becoming a lorry driver — or failing that, an astronaut. As it turns out, he got stuck behind a drawing board, so sometimes he draws articulated lorries and space shuttles. Igor makes a living as an illustrator. Most of his work involves illustrating books for children. He lives in Ljubljana, Slovenia.